W9-CMJ-444

Time
OUT!

Philomel Books
an imprint of Penguin Random House LLC
375 Hudson Street
New York, NY 10014

Copyright © 2017 by Ale Barba.
Penguin supports copyright. Copyright fuels creativity, encourages diverse voices, promotes free speech, and creates a vibrant culture. Thank you for buying an authorized edition of this book and for complying with copyright laws by not reproducing, scanning, or distributing any part of it in any form without permission. You are supporting writers and allowing Penguin to continue to publish books for every reader.

Philomel Books is a registered trademark of Penguin Random House LLC.

Library of Congress Cataloging-in-Publication Data is available upon request.

Manufactured in China by RR Donnelley Asia Printing Solutions Ltd.
ISBN 9780399163043
10 9 8 7 6 5 4 3 2 1

Edited by Jill Santopolo.
Design by Ellice M. Lee.
Text set in Cachet Std.
The art was made using acrylics and cotton paper.

Author's note: Making this book was a fantastic journey, thank you Semadar and Jill.

To Andres, Vero, and their big noses.

Some enchanted evening . . .

Ale Barba

TIME

OUT!
PHILOMEL BOOKS

Sh!

That's IT!

You're in Time Out.

Stay right there until I tell you that you can leave.

Did you **hear** me?

What's going on in there?

FOUR

minutes left.

I want you to think about what you've done.

And **not move**

a muscle!

CHOCO

TWO
minutes left!

I hope you're
really
thinking about it.

Okay,

time's up.

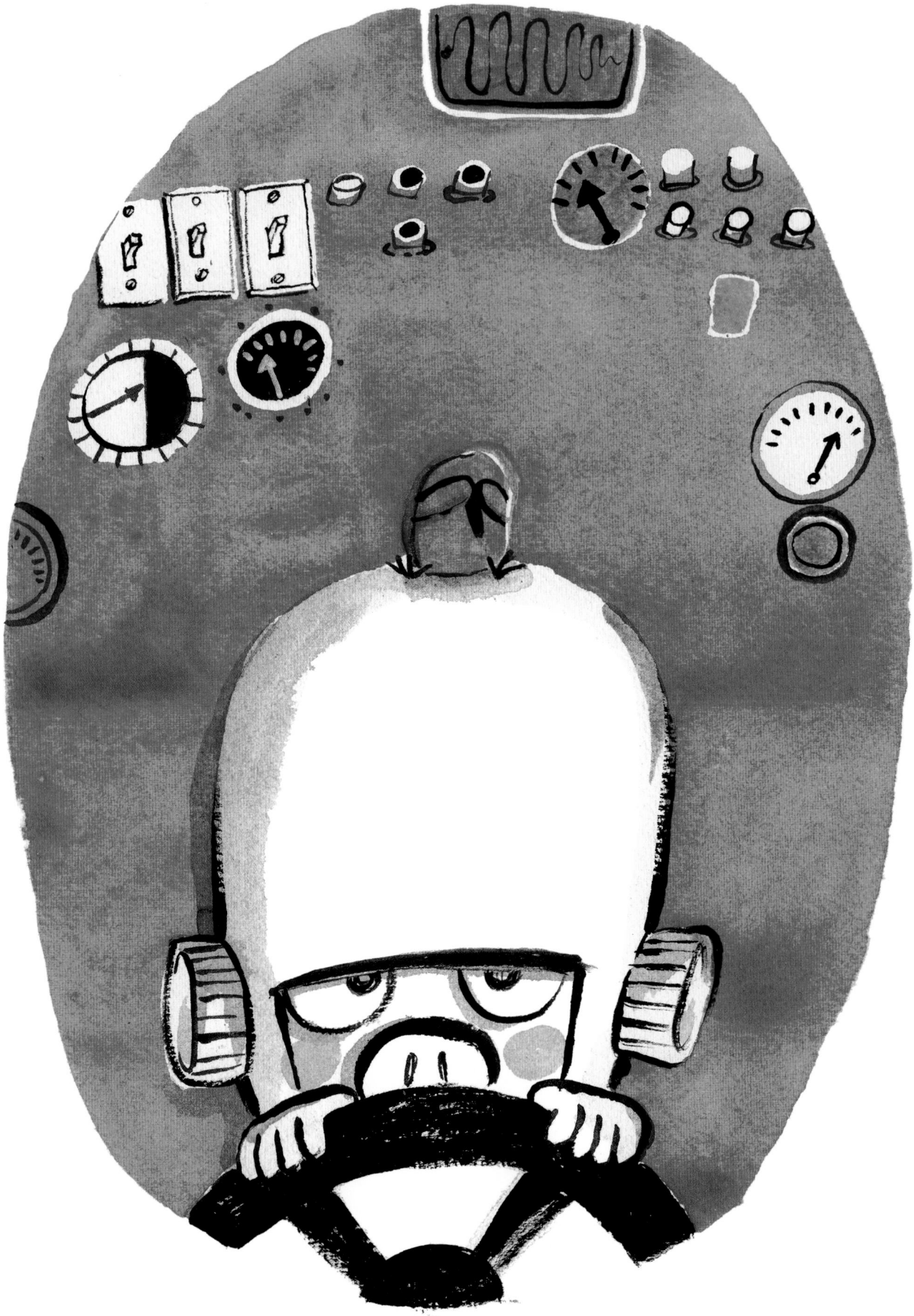

You can come out now.

You did such a good job behaving yourself.
ROCK
CONCERT

Here's your
skateboard back.

TIME IN.

E BARBA
Barba, Ale,
Time out! /

FLT

07/17